The Magical, Mystical Book of EVERYTHING

By Dona Herweck Rice
Illustrated by Luke Scriven

Publishing Credits

Rachelle Cracchiolo, M.S.Ed., *Publisher*
Conni Medina, M.A.Ed., *Editor in Chief*
Nika Fabienke, Ed.D., *Content Director*
Véronique Bos, *Creative Director*
Shaun N. Bernadou, *Art Director*
Susan Daddis, M.A.Ed., *Editor*
John Leach, *Assistant Editor*
Jess Johnson, *Graphic Designer*

Image Credits

Illustrated by Luke Scriven

Library of Congress Cataloging-in-Publication Data

Names: Rice, Dona, author. | Scriven, Luke, illustrator.
Title: The magical, mystical book of everything / by Dona Herweck Rice ;
   illustrated by Luke Scriven.
Description: Huntington Beach, CA : Teacher Created Materials, [2020] |
   Includes book club questions. | Audience: Age 12. | Audience: Grades
   4-6.
Identifiers: LCCN 2019026025 (print) | LCCN 2019026026 (ebook) | ISBN
   9781644913345 (paperback) | ISBN 9781644914243 (electronic)
Subjects: LCSH: Readers (Elementary) | Books and reading--Juvenile fiction.
   | Families--Juvenile fiction.
Classification: LCC PE1119 .R4657 2020 (print) | LCC PE1119 (ebook) | DDC
   428.6/2--dc23
LC record available at https://lccn.loc.gov/2019026025
LC ebook record available at https://lccn.loc.gov/2019026026

5301 Oceanus Drive
Huntington Beach, CA 92649-1030
www.tcmpub.com

ISBN 978-1-6449-1334-5

Printed in Malaysia. THU001.8400

Table of Contents

CHAPTER ONE

※

A New Day

"Ahh, that hits the spot.
Does it not?"
The tiny, gray-haired woman of
uncertain age sat sipping her morning
tea. She set down her teacup with a
satisfying clink on its matching saucer.

"I wonder who—I mean what—*is in store for us today.*
Felis, my dear, what do you say?"

Mrs. Bibliogo stretched the crooked joints of her wrinkled hand along the tabby fur of the contented library cat. Felis purred in agreement. Each day always brought a new seeker. And Mrs. B always knew exactly what that seeker truly sought. She kept it handy in the creaky, old cabinet behind the reference counter. The cabinet had weird etchings of wizards, wands, and moonlight, if one cared to look closely enough. Which Felis did not, thank you very much. He was just fine where he was, plopped comfortably on Mrs. B's blanket-covered lap.

"Well, we'll be ready when they come. Won't we, little furry one?"

"Surrrrre," Felis purred in reply.

"That's my witty kitty."

CHAPTER TWO

⚛

Enter Rosie

Rosie turned right off Bleecker Street onto 7th Avenue, lugging her heavy backpack. She was headed home from school to where her family lived above Popolchek's Bakery.

"Hi, *Bubbee*," Rosie called as she opened the bakery's screen door, ringing the bell overhead.

Rosie's grandmother looked up from the counter where she was helping Mr. Kapowitz buy his daily raisin babka.

"Hello, *bubeleh*," Bubbee said with a warm smile. "Have a snack, and then put on your apron. We have a special order of macaroons to bake right away."

Rosie smiled at Bubbee but groaned inside. Ugh! She did *not* like working at the bakery. It had been in her family since long before Rosie was born. All her friends got to go home after school, get their homework done, and then just hang out doing whatever. But not her—she had to work in this stupid, smelly bakery. Okay, it didn't smell. Well, it smelled pretty great actually.

She would never tell Bubbee how she felt. Bubbee loved this place. The whole family did.

"Okay, Bubbee, I'll come in a minute," Rosie called, heading up the side stairway to the family's upstairs apartment. Unlocking the door and stepping inside, she heard her parents in the kitchen. It sounded like they were arguing about something.

"Oh, great," Rosie whispered under her breath. But she froze where she was, trying to listen in without alerting them that she was there. It might be something interesting, and they always thought she was too little to know things.

"She's got to learn, Miriam. She has no idea what they went through, and she takes it all for granted," Rosie heard her father say.

"I know, I know. But do you really think it's best? That old woman scared me to death when I was a kid. I mean, she's a little spooky, don't you think? And how old is she anyway? She had to be 100 years old 20 years ago!" Rosie's mother clearly didn't agree with whatever her dad wanted.

"All I know is, she changed everything for me in ways I still don't understand—it's all a little fuzzy—but I know it worked."

"The fact that it's fuzzy makes me nervous! I mean, what really happened to you?" Mom took a breath and then added hesitantly, "Okay, okay, I know you believe it changed your life, and I believe you. All right, Samuel, if you think it's best, I'll agree to it. I just hope you know what you're doing."

This doesn't sound very good, Rosie thought. She turned around quickly to backtrack out the door, but her swinging backpack jolted the umbrella stand. The umbrellas clattered, and Rosie winced.

"Traitors!" she hissed at them.

"Rosie, is that you? Come here, honey," her mom called.

I'm doomed, Rosie thought, heading for the kitchen, dragging her backpack behind her.

CHAPTER THREE

⚛

To the Library!

In the end, what Rosie's parents told her really wasn't all that bad. They were sending her to the library. It actually sounded pretty great! She didn't have to make the macaroons, and she got to check out some good books to read.

Of course, nothing with her parents was totally easy. Before she left, she did have to listen to a long lecture on their family history. What that had to do with anything, she wasn't sure. But her dad wanted her to remember that she was named for her great-great-grandmother, the original Rosie Popolchek.

He reminded her, too, how all the family kept the Popolchek name over time—men and women alike. And the bakery was passed down from Popolchek to Popolchek. Rosie gave it to her son, Satchel, who gave it to his daughter, Sadie—Bubbee. Bubbee gave it to Rosie's dad, Samuel. And Dad hoped to give it to Rosie one day. (Not if Rosie could help it!)

"Okay, okay," Rosie huffed. "Can I go to the library now?"

Mom gave Rosie a look that had her changing her expression immediately. She could tell Mom meant business, but Dad looked sad.

"Sure, go," he said, "But be sure to check in with Mrs. Bibliogo when you get there. She has a book for you."

"Got it, Dad," Rosie said as positively as she could manage and then kissed Dad's cheek. She kissed Mom, too, and then out the door she ran before they could change their minds.

"Bye, Bubbee!" she called as she dashed out the bakery door.

The library was just a few blocks away near Washington Square Park. She walked through the heavy front door and stepped eagerly through the turnstile, ready to explore.

"Miss Popolchek, I presume. How are you this afternoon?"

Rosie jumped and spun around. She was nearly nose to nose with a tiny woman sporting a tight gray bun on top of her head. The woman wore a neat, blue sweater set, matching wool skirt, pantyhose, and sensible black shoes. In contrast to all this fussiness, bedazzled reading glasses hung from a beaded chain around her neck.

"I-I-I'm fine," Rosie stuttered and cleared her throat. "Are you Mrs. Bib... Biblio...Bibliogogo?"

"Just one 'go,' dear," Mrs. Bibliogo corrected with a tight smile and a raised eyebrow.

"But you may call me Mrs. B.
All my friends do, you see.
Please follow me to the reference desk,
as your parents have made a
special request."

Then, she crooked her finger in front of Rosie's startled face. Mrs. B spun around, military style, and headed toward the reference counter.

Rosie willed her feet to move and stumbled along behind her. "Coming," she mumbled.

⁂

CHAPTER FOUR

Everything You Were Looking For

Mrs. B slowly made her way around the library counter. A chubby tabby cat lounged atop a cabinet behind her, its eyes following the tiny woman.
"Have a seat, my dear.
The perfect spot you'll find right here."

She gestured her hand toward a small table at the end of the counter.

Rosie looked toward the table and wrinkled her brow. *It looks harmless enough,* she thought. *Mrs. B is a little weird, but what could happen in the middle of the library?* She nodded at Mrs. B and made her way to the table.

Glancing down, Rosie noticed a cool etching in the tabletop. It was faded, but she could just make out some kind of wizard holding a wand under a giant moon.

Rosie glanced at Mrs. B, who was just then reaching up to her pointy bun and pulling out a bobby pin. *Or maybe it's not a bobby pin*, Rosie thought when she saw Mrs. B use it to unlock the top of an old wooden cabinet behind the counter.

Mrs. B reached up and gingerly pulled down a leather-bound book, old and worn from use. She looked at Rosie with a knowing smile. Rosie felt a chill creep down her spine. *What is up with this lady?* she wondered.

Mrs. B slowly toddled over to Rosie and plopped the book on her table.

*"My dear, I believe this
is the book you need.
You'll find everything
you were looking for when you read."*

"But I wasn't looking for anything," Rosie replied with frustration. "My parents sent—"

*"Yes, indeed.
Read."*

Mrs. B raised her eyebrow as she tapped the cover with her finger.

Rosie opened her mouth to argue but, noting the look on Mrs. B's face, swallowed her words and looked down at the book. Opening the fragile, old cover, she read the title on the first page: *The Magical, Mystical Book of Everything.*

Okay, that's cool, Rosie thought, turning the page.

And then the world went black.

A casual library-goer would see only a girl sitting at a desk, her head bent over a battered, old book and her hair hanging down the sides of her face. The book was open to the first page. If they looked closer, they might notice that not a single word or picture was on it. It was perfectly empty! And yet Rosie seemed fascinated. She wasn't moving at all. In fact, she was absolutely entranced. Literally.

Rosie's body sat at the desk, but Rosie herself was not there. She was wandering around inside the pages of the book, wondering where she was and how in the world she had gotten there.

CHAPTER FIVE

⊠

Inside the Book

Rosie rubbed her eyes, which had gone fuzzy, and she felt a tingling from her head to her toes. She blinked to clear her vision, but when she opened her eyes, the world around her was different—and yet the same. She was standing on the familiar corner of 7th and Bleecker. There were no traffic

lights though, and there were no cars or buses. But there *were* horses and wagons! And although there were plenty of people, they were all dressed funny in old-timey suits and long dresses with high necks and puffy sleeves. Everyone had a hat on—even the kids! It was like Rosie had stepped into a really old photograph come to life.

But wait a minute! Up ahead there was a sign—one Rosie knew very well. "Popolchek's Bakery," it read. Rosie had to see it up close for herself.

Rosie stepped inside the screen door, the bell ringing overhead as the woman behind the counter greeted her. She had a warm face and twinkling eyes that reminded Rosie of Bubbee.

"Hello, *bubeleh*," the woman said with a thick Yiddish accent. "What can I get you?"

Rosie was bewildered. This bakery was her family's bakery, but it looked so strange. Baked goods were unwrapped on open shelves, gaslights lined the walls, and a big metal machine with buttons and a lever sat on the countertop. But even so, Rosie knew this place like the back of her hand.

"Can you tell me, ma'am, what's your name?" Rosie asked, her heart in her throat.

"I am Rosie Popolchek," the woman said brightly, "and this is my new bakery. How do you like it?"

"I...I...," Rosie started to say, but then she turned and ran out the door. Rosie Popolchek...her great-great-grandmother? How could that be?

Rosie's head started spinning and her vision blurred again. When she opened her eyes, she was in a noisy factory. Huge metal sewing machines lined the walls, and worn-out women were bent over their work. Young children dashed about everywhere, poorly dressed and exhausted. They were moving bolts of cloth, threading machines, and performing all sorts of repetitive tasks. Rosie wondered why

they weren't in school. The place was sweltering, dusty, and loud, and Rosie couldn't wait to leave.

Turning to go, she bumped into a familiar face—much younger than before. It was Grandmother Rosie as a child!

"What are you doing here?" Rosie asked.

"What am I doing? I'm working. My family needs to eat, don't they?" she said hurriedly.

"But why aren't you in school?"

"School? Who can afford to go to school? We work every hour we're not sleeping. But one day—one day, I will save all my pennies, and I will open a bakery and serve the finest babka. I will take care of my family and save us from this life. You'll see!" she said with conviction.

"I believe you," Rosie agreed before the world started spinning again.